jP AUC

Auch, Mary Jane.
The plot chickens.

THE PLOT CHICKENS

Mary Jane and Herm Auch

Holiday House / New York

*For Joy Davia Auch,
who brings joy into
our lives*

*Special thanks to author/illustrator
Janie Bynum, who gave us
the title for this book*

Text copyright © 2009 by Mary Jane Auch
Illustrations copyright © 2009 by Mary Jane and Herm Auch
All Rights Reserved
Printed and Bound in China
The text typeface is Pink Martini.
The artwork for this book was created with a combination
of oil paints and digital technology.
www.holidayhouse.com
First Edition
1 3 5 7 9 10 8 6 4 2

Library of Congress Cataloging-in-Publication Data
Auch, Mary Jane.
The plot chickens / by Mary Jane Auch. – 1st ed.
p. cm.
Summary: Henrietta the chicken loves to read so much that she decides
to write a book herself, but first no one will publish a book written by a chicken,
and then, when she publishes it herself and it gets a terrible review
in "The Corn Book," Henrietta is devastated.
ISBN-13: 978-0-8234-2087-2 (hardcover)
[1. Chickens–Fiction. 2. Authorship–Fiction. 3. Humorous stories.] I. Title.
PZ7.A898Pl 2008
[E]–dc22
2007011234

Henrietta loved to read. Soon she had read every
book on the farm a dozen times, so she went to town
to find more. When she spotted people carrying books
out of the library, she went inside to wait in line.

When it was Henrietta's turn, the librarian said,
"We have nothing for chickens here.
Try the feed store."
Frustrated, Henrietta
clucked at the top
of her lungs,

BUK, BUK,
BUK!

"Well, why didn't
you say so?"
The librarian handed
her three books.

Henrietta was
in reading eggstasy.
Every day she read
to her aunts, then
returned the books
to the library for
more.

MORISSA

GOLDA

LIZ

One day Henrietta said, "Reading books is so much fun. Writing books must be eggshilarating." She searched the shelves until she found a book about writing. The librarian was impressed.

When she got home, Henrietta read,
"RULE ONE: You need a main character."

Aunt Golda won
because she was the oldest.
Henrietta found a
typewriter and began to
peck out a story.

Once upon a
time there was a
hen named Aunt
Golda.

Hunt & Peck

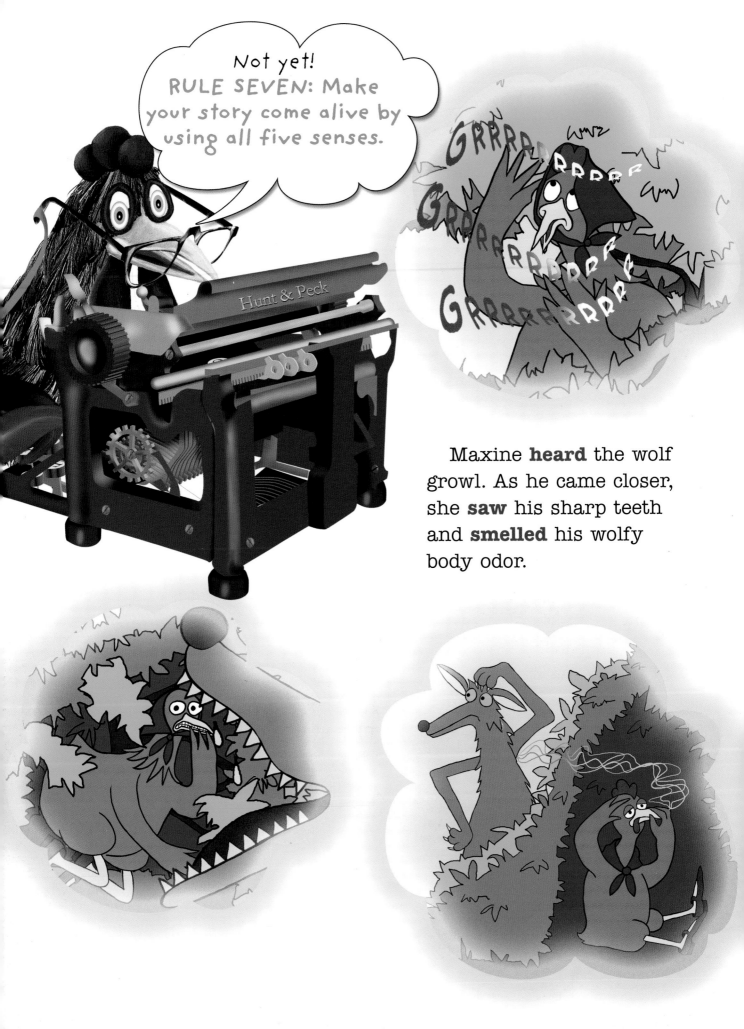

Not yet!
RULE SEVEN: Make your story come alive by using all five senses.

Maxine **heard** the wolf growl. As he came closer, she **saw** his sharp teeth and **smelled** his wolfy body odor.

When he was nearer still, she **felt** the heat of his icky breath.

When he stuck his head through the leaves, Maxine **tasted** the bile rising from her gizzard.

Then Maxine dies of fright. THE END. Good story.

That is *not* THE END! Endings are the hardest part.

Maxine gathered her courage. Then she plunged her sharp beak into the tip of the wolf's tender nose. The wolf howled in pain and ran off, never to be seen again. THE END.

Good story.

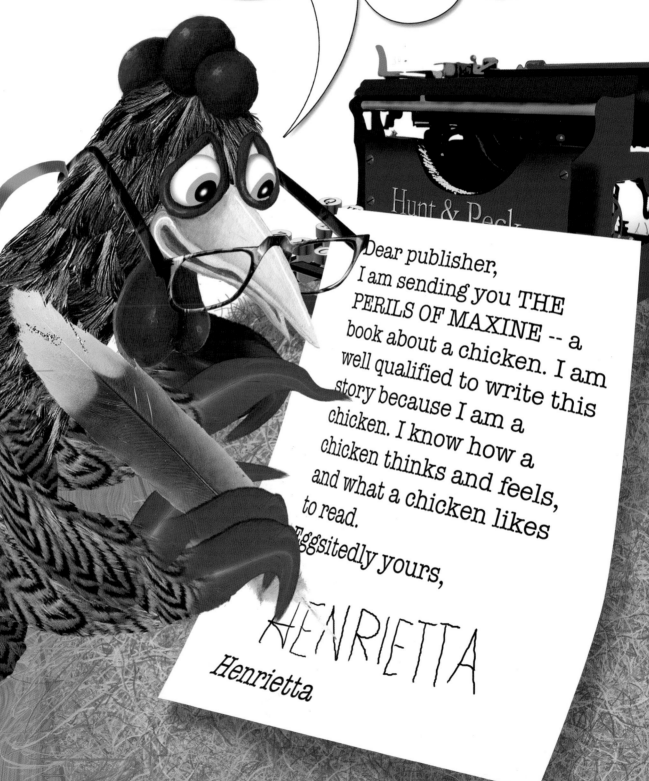

Many, many, many months later, the publisher sent a rejection letter.

Fox Publishing

Ms. Henrietta,
Brewster Farms
Niceville, USA

Dear Ms. Henrietta:
We do not publish books written by chickens. Even if we did, we wouldn't want this one. We didn't like it.

Don't quit your day job. Have a nice life.

Hunter Fox, Editor

The aunts were devastated, but Henrietta vowed not to brood over her rejection.

Yellow

Yellow plus Magenta

Yellow, Magenta, plus Cyan

Yellow, Magenta, Cyan, plus Black

When her books were finished, Henrietta gave one
to the librarian.

"Your book should be reviewed,"
the librarian said. "Send it to
The Corn Book."

So Henrietta mailed it off.

When *The Corn Book* review came out, it said:

Henrietta *The Perils of Maxine*
One Dozen Pages   Cider Press

Henrietta lays an egg with her first book. We hope this is her last book. *The Perils of Maxine* shows why chickens shouldn't EVER write. It is odoriferous.   Noah Lyke

Odoriferous means it stinks. End of story.

"I'm going to keep writing," Henrietta said, but her feelings were hurt. And a little voice inside her kept saying . . .

Henrietta's heart wasn't into writing anymore. She even stopped going to the library. But her aunts missed hearing Henrietta read, so they bugged her until she went to get some books.

Henrietta was embarrassed. Had the librarian seen that awful review?

When Henrietta went into the story room,
the children cheered. She read with dramatic
expression. Of course, all the children heard was

BUK BUK

BUK

BUK BUK

BUK

BUK

but it didn't matter.
They knew the story
by heart.

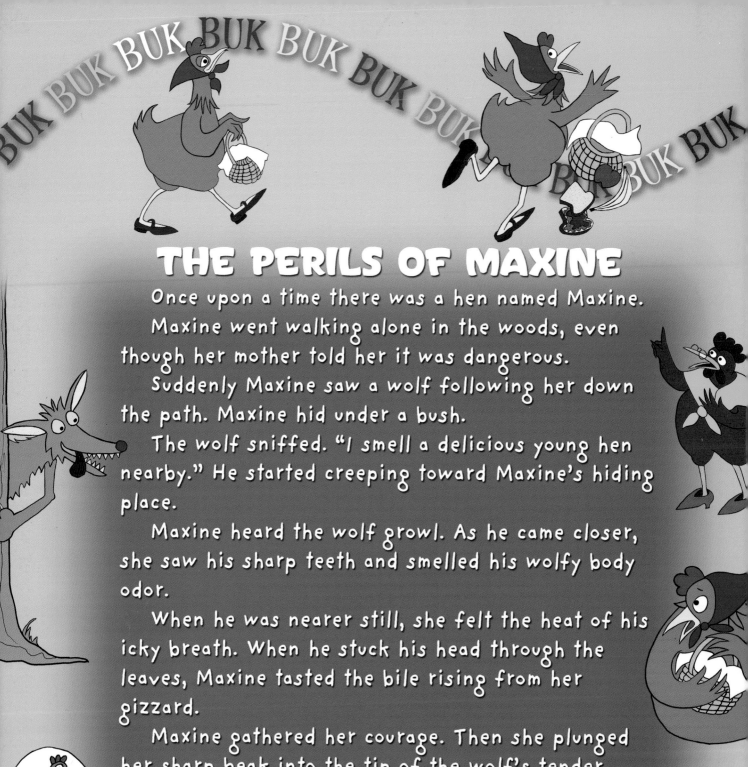

THE PERILS OF MAXINE

Once upon a time there was a hen named Maxine. Maxine went walking alone in the woods, even though her mother told her it was dangerous.

Suddenly Maxine saw a wolf following her down the path. Maxine hid under a bush.

The wolf sniffed. "I smell a delicious young hen nearby." He started creeping toward Maxine's hiding place.

Maxine heard the wolf growl. As he came closer, she saw his sharp teeth and smelled his wolfy body odor.

When he was nearer still, she felt the heat of his icky breath. When he stuck his head through the leaves, Maxine tasted the bile rising from her gizzard.

Maxine gathered her courage. Then she plunged her sharp beak into the tip of the wolf's tender nose. The wolf howled in pain and ran off, never to be seen again.

THE END.